FAIR!

★ TED LEWIN *★*

Lothrop, Lee & Shepard Books • Morrow
New York

To Judge John and Mary Ann Reilly
and the good people of Clearfield, Pennsylvania

Published by Lothrop, Lee & Shepard Books
an imprint of Morrow Junior Books
a division of William Morrow & Company, Inc.
1350 Avenue of the Americas, New York, NY 10019

Printed in the United States of America.

1 2 3 4 5 6 7 8 9 10

Library of Congress Cataloging-in-Publication Data
Lewin, Ted.
Fair!/Ted Lewin.
p. cm.
Summary: Describes the sights, sounds, and smells of a county fair, from the setting up of the Ferris wheel to the animal, craft, and food judging.
ISBN 0-688-12850-5 (trade)—ISBN 0-688-12851-3 (library)
1. Fairs—United States—Juvenile literature. 2. United States—Social life and customs—Juvenile literature.
[1. Fairs.] I. Title. GT4603.A2L49 1997 394'.6'0973—dc21 96-51146 CIP AC

In the valley lies an empty fairground, waiting. All year its long sheds have been empty, waiting for the farm animals. Its great exposition hall has been empty, waiting to be filled with jams and jellies, fruits and flowers, cakes and quilts. Its grandstand bleachers have been empty, waiting for the cheering crowds. All waiting for the big day when the carnival rolls in; all waiting for the county fair.

Huge carnival trucks, on the road all night, bring in the rides and the sideshow. They've just come in from Smithport, and before that Churchville, and before that Stoneboro, Sykesville, and Harbor Creek. "So many towns, you forget where you're at," the drivers say.

In come the rides: Pink Panther, Sky Diver, Loopo Plane, Swinger. As the
sun breaks through the clouds, they unfold from their truckbeds like giant
metal insects emerging from cocoons. Bare-chested roustabouts, just back
from their coffee at Beech's Big Boy, swarm over them. Up go the Fun Haus,
the Ferris Wheel, the Tilt-a-Whirl, and the Flying Bobs.

They have traveled three thousand miles so far this season, with a thousand more to go. Soon thirty trucks are in the fairground and a hundred roustabouts are sorting and assembling the pieces of this giant jigsaw puzzle. Electric cables are spread on the ground like spaghetti. Countless thousands of lightbulbs have to be replaced in every town.

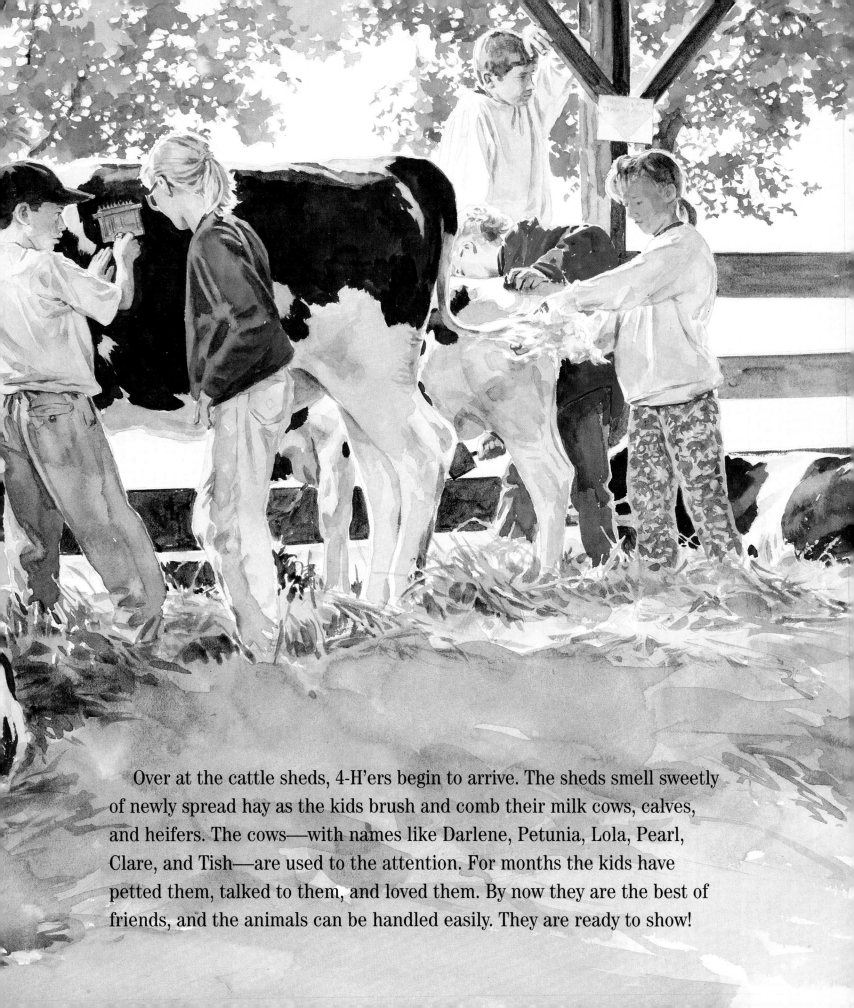

Over at the cattle sheds, 4-H'ers begin to arrive. The sheds smell sweetly of newly spread hay as the kids brush and comb their milk cows, calves, and heifers. The cows—with names like Darlene, Petunia, Lola, Pearl, Clare, and Tish—are used to the attention. For months the kids have petted them, talked to them, and loved them. By now they are the best of friends, and the animals can be handled easily. They are ready to show!

Outside the sheep sheds, whole families help to scrub the sheep, clip them, fluff their tails, and sometimes blacken their hooves and noses with shoe polish. The kids got their lambs the first of May and have had exactly ninety days to train them for show. The lambs have grown fast, gaining a pound a day from mother's milk and grass, and are as loving and loyal to their trainers as dogs.

Southdowns, Suffolks, Hampshires, and Oxfords will all be judged for length and width of loin and size of leg and back end. Fresh from the shearing stands, they are wrapped in canvas blankets and hoods to keep them clean.

Trailers bursting with pigs back up to the swine shed, and farmers drive the pigs into the chute—Hampshires, Berkshires, Landraces, and Spotteds, all squealing like banshees. Horses, poultry, pigeons, and rabbits are arriving at other sheds to be brushed and combed and pampered like kings and queens. The exposition hall is filling with jams and jellies, quilts and leatherwork, prize fruits and vegetables, cakes and pies and pickles, wood carvings and metalwork.

It's here at last—opening day! In late afternoon, the parade forms at the far end of town and strikes out across the old trestle bridge, state trooper color guard in the lead. Behind them the hometown high school band, one hundred fifty strong. On and on they come, bands and fire engines and floats from every town in the county, past the cheering throngs that line the street and finally onto the fairground track.

The grandstand is jam-packed with spectators from all over the county. A roar goes up for the fair queen and the dairy princess, waving from atop their float pulled by an old Farmall tractor. A vintage steamer drawn by a team of Belgians glints in the last rays of the sun.

The sun sets as the last band passes. The crowd is hushed, knowing what's next. Then suddenly the silence explodes with pops and bangs and whistles, and the sky fills with a fireworks extravaganza.

At last the crowd pours out into the midway, where a bastion of food stands has magically appeared. Steak-on-a-stick, sno-cones, funnel cakes, and wing dings. Curly fries, elephant ears, and chili dogs. The crowd wanders through the carnival, eating all the while. Sugar waffles, buffalo burgers, and caramel corn.

People play Fat Albert, Shoot the Hoop, and win a Goldfish. They have their weight guessed and their strength tested. They ride the Cyclone and the Ferris Wheel and the Tilt-a-Whirl.

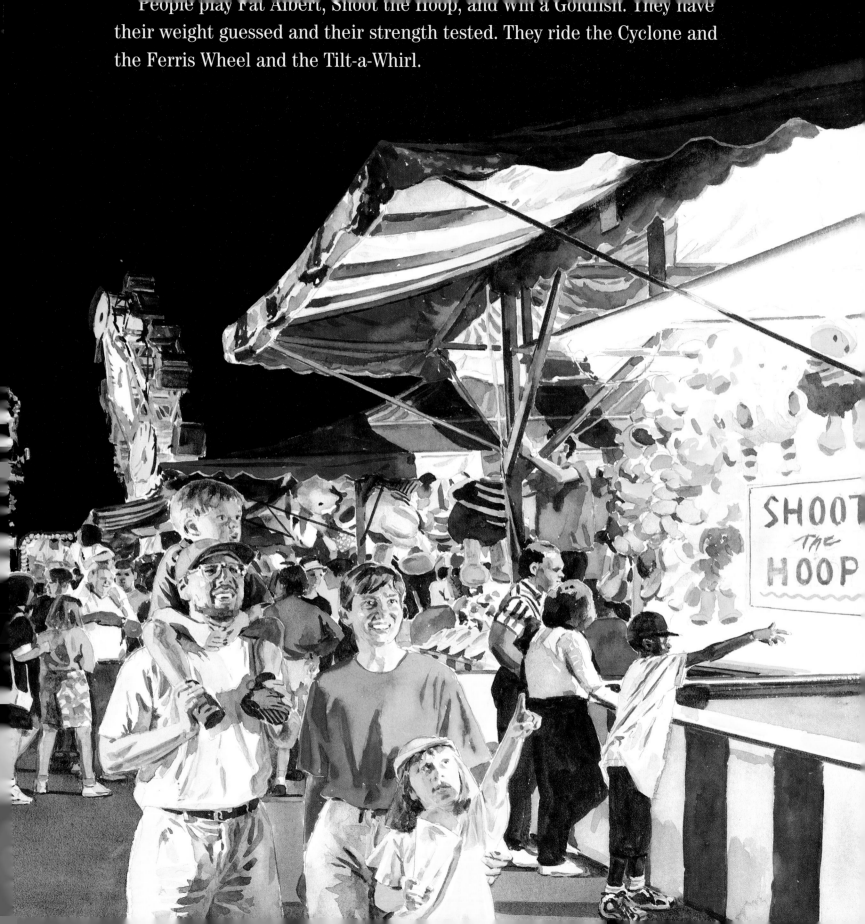

Above the din, a voice drones over the loudspeaker:
Step right up and see the Fish Girl. Blown in on a Louisiana hurricane. Is she human, or is she fish? Ever seen an animal with two heads? Well, we have three of 'em. A rabbit with two heads from Wisconsin. A pig with two heads from Tennessee. And a raccoon with two heads from Pennsylvania. It's amazing! It's incredible. And it's educational!

At last the crowd begins to thin. Parents carry sleepy children to their cars and home to bed. Farmers head for their trailers. 4-H'ers head for the barns to check once more on their animals and some to spend the night. Tomorrow is a big day—the judging will begin.

For the next four days, quilts and crafts, fruit and flowers and vegetables will all be judged in the exposition hall. Cabbages, string beans, and squash will be judged for size, shape, and color; breads, cakes, and pies for flavor, lightness, and crumb. Jellies, jams, and butters in standard clear jars; pickles—sweet, dill, and mustard; African violets and waxed begonias, lovingly tended all year long; clothing, needlework, rugs, photography, and wood carvings are all here to be judged. Even if no prize is won, everyone takes pride in a job well done.

The judging of animals goes on for four days, too. In the cattle shed, the judge instructs the junior showmen: "Keep your eyes on me at all times and the animal looking at me, with her head in the air, looking the best she can, moving smoothly like she's in a beauty pageant. This *is* her beauty pageant."

The judge studies the heifers—the shape of their heads, the texture of their skin, their backs and legs and feet—and picks a winner. Then the dairy princess hands out the ribbons: yellow for fifth place, pink for fourth, white for third, red for second, and, best of all, the first-prize blue. Come winter, when the fair is just a memory, those ribbons will still be fresh, carefully preserved in their proud owners' memory books.

Before the pigs are shown, they have been fussed over like movie stars, dark ones rubbed with baby oil until they gleam, white ones dusted with baby powder until they glow. They squeal past the sharp-eyed judge, kept in line by showmen with stout wooden canes in one hand and brushes in the other for quick touch-ups.

Over at the grandstand, the horse pulling has started. Farmers ride the doubletrees like chariot drivers; their sixteen-hundred-pound horses prance onto the track with dainty little steps. The horses are keyed up and can't wait to pull a sledge full of cinder blocks that can weigh eight thousand pounds. The moment the mighty team hears the doubletree being attached to the sledge, it lurches forward. Hooves dig in, nostrils flare, dirt flies, chains clank, and leather squeaks and strains. The sledge begins to move!

As the week draws to a close, chunky ponies, saddle horses, and giant draft horses have their moments. Shetland and Welsh ponies, Appaloosas, Morgans, and Arabians, and the huge Clydesdales, Suffolks, and Belgians with their meticulously braided tails, all swing their hips before the judges. Finally, the sweet reward of a blue ribbon.

Nearby, in a tent next to Madame Fatima the palm reader, for fifty cents you can see "the world's largest cow—ten thousand hamburgers on the hoof." Inside in the gloom, a child with the face of an angel leans against the warm bulk of the great beast and hums softly.

Tomorrow this will all be gone, and the fairground will again be empty and still. The animals will be back in their pastures and farmyards. The proud 4-H'ers will be savoring the last days of summer.

And the carnival workers will be off to another fairground in Waldenville, then Johnstown, then Lewiston. "So many towns, you forget where you're at."